HAL'S magical BUBBLES

A Lesson on Gratitude

By: Lindsey Lee Lamb

Illustrated by: Stephanie de la Cruz

This book belongs to:

FIRST EDITION October 2020

Book written by Lindsey Lee Lamb
Book illustrations by Stephanie de la Cruz
Illustrations dedicated to Joy de la Cruz and Reef

Special thanks to Tamara Beach and Sarah Woods.

ISBN 978-1-7355643-1-9 (paperback & ebook)

Published by Lindsey Lee Lamb Books
www.lindseyleelamb.com

For Harper,
may you always find joy and stay curious.
I love you.

For Bella,
your spunky spirit will never be forgotten.

It's morning! I wake with a big yawn.
My parents must not know it's dawn.

I walk down the hall and wake them
up. I remind them we must let out
my Pup.

A morning we don't walk Pup is rare.
And today I'll make her a panda bear!

I'm tired of Pup, as you can tell. So,
I'll blow bubbles on her as a spell.

Voila! **A panda she will become, and
I'm sure our walk will be more fun.**

After breakfast, we head outside.
We set up my stroller for a ride!

Mom grabs Pup's leash and looks around. Of course, Pup is nowhere to be found! Instead, there sits a large panda bear. My parents leash her without a care!

We start our walk and I'm so excited!
I'm sure my new panda is also delighted.

However, soon things take a funny turn. Panda
has walking etiquette to learn. We pass a
neighbor's house with trees. The look on
Panda's face says, *"Yes, please!"*

**Without warning, Panda climbs
up quick. My parents seem
unimpressed with her trick.**

She sits there awhile, looking around. Soon, she realizes there is no bamboo to be found!

Down she climbs with a frown on her face. Off to the next tree we race!

We do this our entire walk, you
see. Finally, the leash breaks and
Panda is free!

To get Panda home takes quite a while… so long that Mom, Dad, nor I can barely smile.

Once home, an idea pops in my head.
I'll blow bubbles on Panda so Pup's here instead!

Thank goodness our Pup is back!
Now our walks will be back on track.

Pup's walking etiquette surpassed Panda's by far. Panda's behavior was not up to par.

When our walk is done, we look at each other and smile. Our walking adventure this morning was pretty wild.

Turning Pup into something else tomorrow would be a breeze. But I'd rather have our family walks go with ease.

**Changing Pup made me realize I love her a
lot. I think it's important to appreciate what
you've got.**

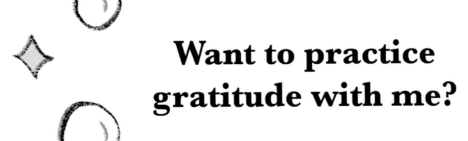

Want to practice gratitude with me?

Gratitude

My name is _____

Today I felt

Today the weather was

The best thing about today	Today I learned

Today I struggled with	Today I helped

I am grateful for

Gratitude

My name is _____

Today I felt

Today the weather was

The best thing
about today

Today I learned

Today I
struggled with

Today I helped

I am grateful for

Gratitude

My name is _____

Today I felt

Today the weather was

The best thing about today

Today I learned

Today I struggled with

Today I helped

I am grateful for

Gratitude

My name is _____

Today I felt

Today the weather was

The best thing
about today

Today I learned

Today I
struggled with

Today I helped

I am grateful for

Made in the USA
Coppell, TX
12 November 2020